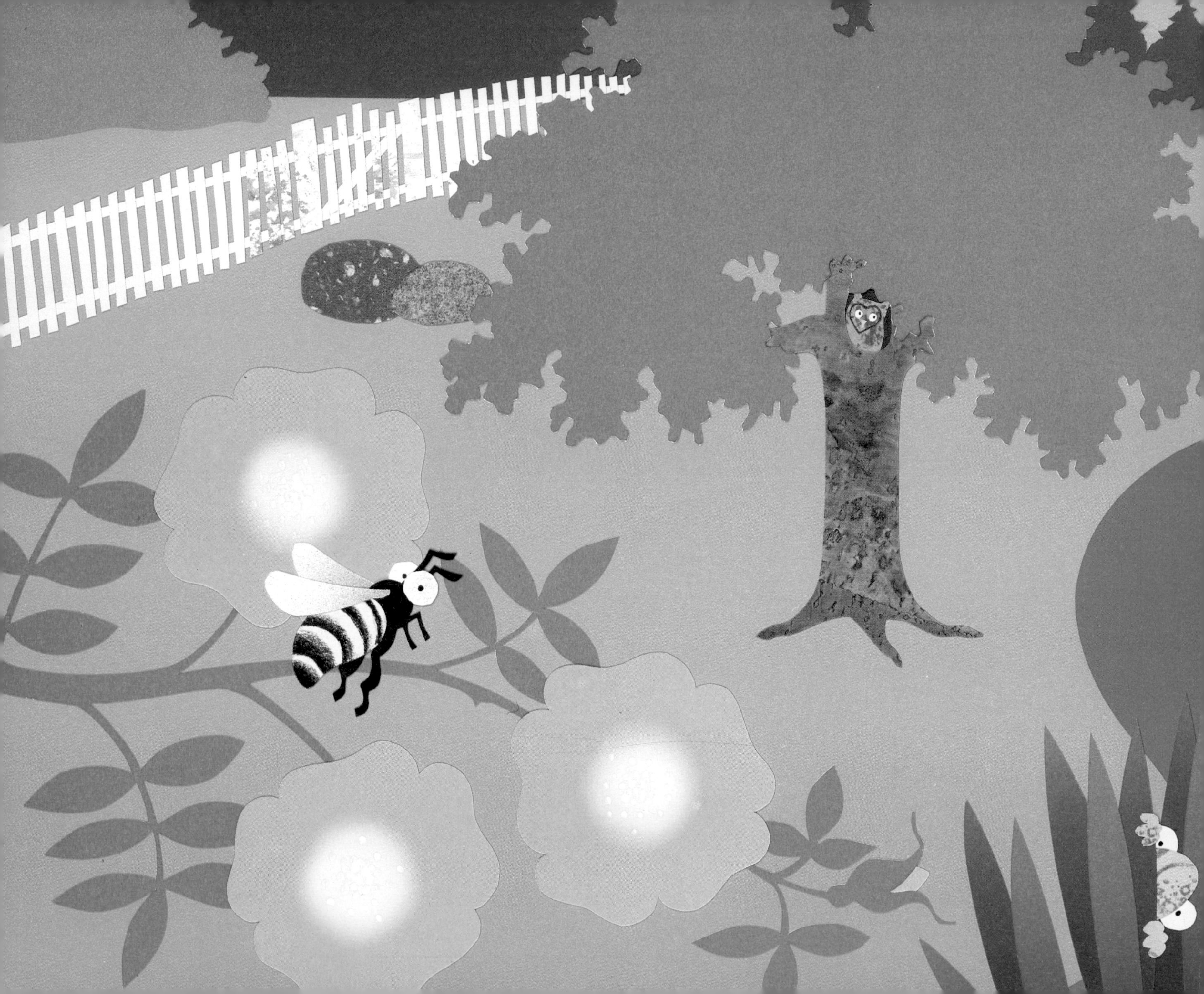

Over in the Meadow

To Margaret, Charles, Leonora, and Joe

0-590-44499-9
ISBN 0-590-29271-4 (meets NASTA specifications)

Illustrations copyright © 1992 by David A. Carter.
All rights reserved. Published by Scholastic Inc.

5 6 7 8 9 10   08   01 00 99 98 97 96 95

Printed in the U.S.A.

Over in the Meadow

An Old Counting Rhyme

(Based on the original by Olive A. Wadsworth)

Illustrated by David A. Carter

SCHOLASTIC INC.

New York Toronto London Auckland Sydney

Over in the meadow in the sand in the sun
Lived an old mother turtle and her little turtle one.
"*Dig*," said the mother. "*We dig*," said the one.
So they dug all day in the sand in the sun.

Over in the meadow where the stream runs blue
Lived an old mother fish and her little fishes two.
"*Swim*," said the mother. "*We swim*," said the two.
So they swam all day where the stream runs blue.

Over in the meadow in the wide oak tree
Lived an old mother owl and her little owls three.
"*Whoo*," said the mother. "*Whoo*," said the three.
So they whooed all day in the wide oak tree.

Over in the meadow by the old barn door
Lived an old mother rat and her little ratties four.
"*Gnaw*," said the mother. "*We gnaw*," said the four.
So they gnawed all day by the old barn door.

Over in the meadow in a snug beehive
Lived an old mother bee and her little bees five.
"*Buzz*," said the mother. "*We buzz*," said the five.
So they buzzed all day round the snug beehive.

Over in the meadow in a nest made of sticks
Lived an old mother crow and her little crows six.
"Caw," said the mother. "*We caw*," said the six.
So they cawed all day in the nest made of sticks.

Over in the meadow where the grass grows even
Lived an old mother frog and her little froggies seven.
"*Jump*," said the mother. "*We jump*," said the seven.
So they jumped all day where the grass grows even.

Over in the meadow by the old mossy gate
Lived an old mother lizard and her little lizards eight.
"*Bask*," said the mother. "*We bask*," said the eight.
So they basked all day by the old mossy gate.

Over in the meadow in the pond by the pine
Swam an old mother duck and her little ducklings nine.
"Quack," said the mother. "We quack," said the nine.
So they quacked all day in the pond by the pine.

Over in the meadow in a cozy wee den
Lived an old mother beaver and her little beavers ten.
"*Build*," said the mother. "*We build*," said the ten.
So they built all day near the cozy wee den.

Over in the meadow in the wide oak tree
Lived an old mother owl and her little owls **three.**
"*Whoo,*" said the mother. "*Whoo,*" said the three.
So they whooed all day in the wide oak tree.

Over in the meadow in the sand in the sun
Lived an old mother turtle and her little turtle **one.**
"*Dig,*" said the mother. "*We dig,*" said the one.
So they dug all day in the sand in the sun.

Over in the meadow by the old barn door
Lived an old mother rat and her little ratties **four.**
"*Gnaw,*" said the mother. "*We gnaw,*" said the four.
So they gnawed all day by the old barn door.

Over in the meadow where the stream runs blue
Lived an old mother fish and her little fishes **two.**
"*Swim,*" said the mother. "*We swim,*" said the two.
So they swam all day where the stream runs blue.

Over in the meadow in a snug beehive
Lived an old mother bee and her little bees **five.**
"*Buzz,*" said the mother. "*We buzz,*" said the five.
So they buzzed all day round the snug beehive.

Over in the meadow in a nest made of sticks
Lived an old mother crow and her little crows **six.**
"Caw," said the mother. "We caw," said the six.
So they cawed all day in the nest made of sticks.

Over in the meadow where the grass grows even
Lived an old mother frog and her little froggies **seven.**
"Jump," said the mother. "We jump," said the seven.
So they jumped all day where the grass grows even.

Over in the meadow by the old mossy gate
Lived an old mother lizard and her little lizards **eight.**
"Bask," said the mother. "We bask," said the eight.
So they basked all day by the old mossy gate.

Over in the meadow in the pond by the pine
Swam an old mother duck and her little ducklings **nine.**
"Quack," said the mother. "We quack," said the nine.
So they quacked all day in the pond by the pine.

Over in the meadow in a cozy wee den
Lived an old mother beaver and her little beavers **ten.**
"Build," said the mother. "We build," said the ten.
So they built all day near the cozy wee den.

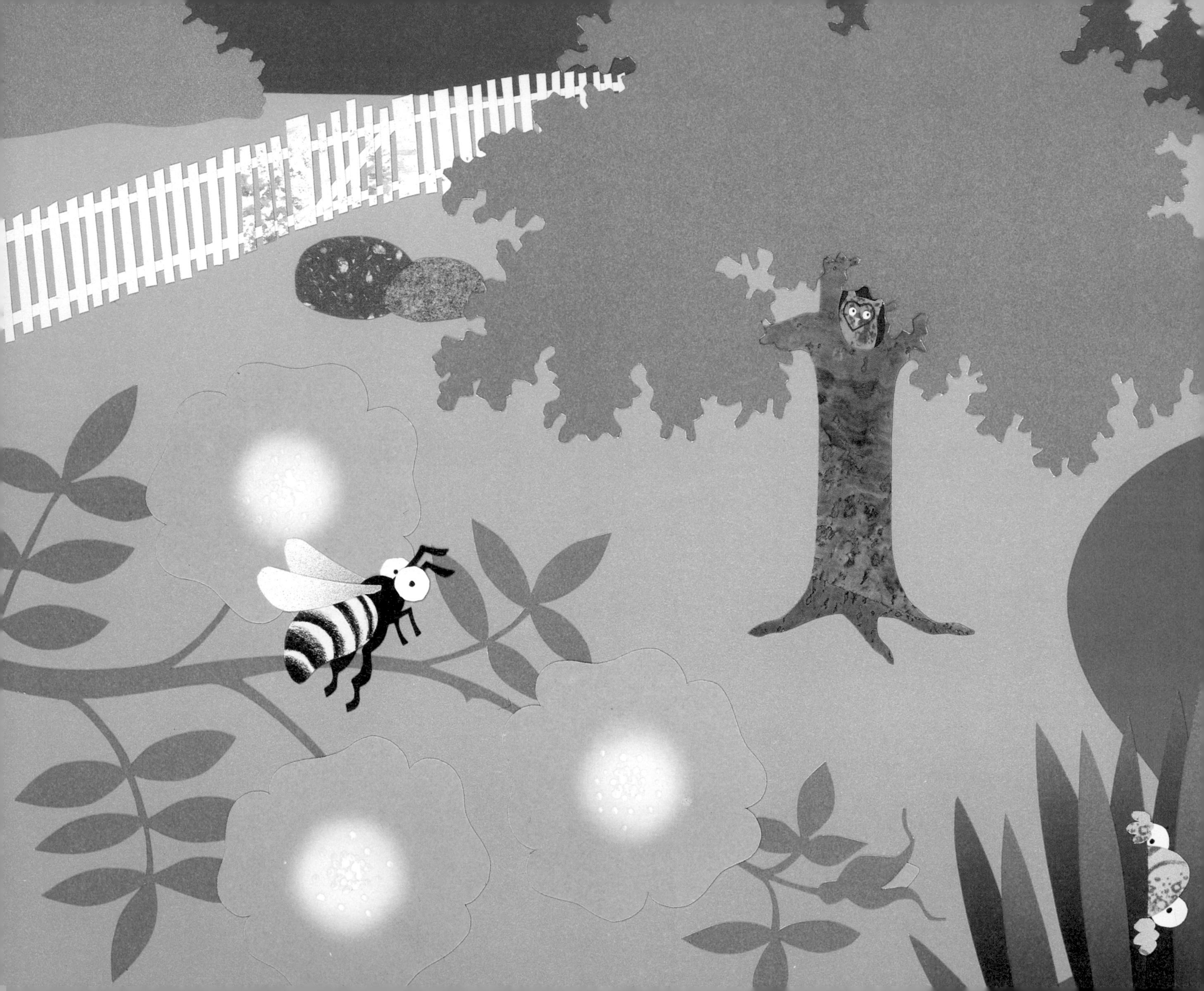